A COSMIC Christmas

By Ken Sobol

AVON CAMELOT

A COSMIC CHRISTMAS
is an original publication of Avon Books.
This work has never before appeared in book form.

"Why Don't They Look To The Stars"
Words and Music by Sylvia Tyson.
Copyright © MCMLXXVIII by Salt Music.

"The Way That Christmas Used To Be"
Words and Music by Sylvia Tyson.
Copyright © MCMLXXVIII by Salt Music.

AVON BOOKS
A division of
The Hearst Corporation
959 Eighth Avenue
New York, New York 10019
Copyright © 1979 by Nelvana Limited
Published by arrangement with Nelvana Limited.
Library of Congress Catalog Card Number: 79-51612
ISBN: 0-380-45930-2

First Camelot Printing, September, 1979

CAMELOT TRADEMARK REG. U.S. PAT. OFF.
AND IN OTHER COUNTRIES, MARCA REGISTRADA,
HECHO EN U.S.A.

Printed in the U.S.A.

Book design by Joan Walton

10   9   8   7   6   5   4   3

CONTENTS

Songs

A Cosmic Christmas

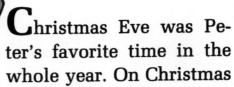Christmas Eve was Peter's favorite time in the whole year. On Christmas Eve his family always sat down to a big dinner. Afterward, friends would come to visit, and they would all sing carols around the tree. Later the family would put their presents under the tree, and Peter would try to guess what his were from the shapes. The only trouble with Christmas Eve was that it took so long to come each year. But today was finally the day.

Early in the afternoon, Peter went downtown to look in the store windows. He paid no attention to the time—until he heard the bells on the town hall clock begin to chime.

Oh, oh. It was five o'clock—and he was supposed to be home by now. Peter lived in the country—not too far out of town, but not so close, either. "Come on, Lucy," he called. "We have to hurry." Lucy was Peter's pet goose.

They started out over the snow-covered fields. Pretty soon they slipped and slid to the edge of Willis Pond. Lucy hopped right out on it, skating across the ice with her webbed feet. But Peter wasn't sure how strong the ice was. After all, winter had just started. Just as he got ready to test it, a voice spoke. "We are approaching the Planet Earth," it said. "Prepare for landing. Prepare for landing."

The voice was coming from above! At first, Peter did not want to look up. He was afraid of what he might see. But then he did, anyway. A glowing white space ball, like a small star, was floating above the treetops. It seemed somehow to be pointing straight down at them. Lucy gave a quack that sounded more like a croak. That meant "Helllllp! It's a spaceship!"

"D-D-D-D-D-Don't   w-w-w-w-worry,

Lucy," stammered Peter. "D-D-D-D-Don't be af-f-f-f-f-f. . . ." He meant to say "afraid," but his teeth were chattering so hard he couldn't get it out. Lucy shot back across the pond and dived behind a big boulder. Peter ran right after her. But after a while he peeked out to see what was happening.

The space ball dipped lower and lower. Mysterious rays shone out from it, turning the snow green and blue and then white again. *Beeps* and *brrrrks* came out, like a radio with a lot of static. It seemed to be looking for a place to land. First it hovered over one spot, then another, then another. Suddenly it turned bright red and sank down to the ground—very near to Peter and Lucy.

They watched fearfully as the space ball settled down and stopped glowing. A moment later, the front door opened (at least Peter thought it was the front door—it might have been the back) and a long, silver pathway unfolded. And out of the still-glimmering insides came three space creatures. One was tall and thin, one was short and fat, and the third was somewhere in between. They all had strange, sharp, ghostly faces, and a

way of moving that made it seem as if the wind were carrying them along. Suddenly a fourth creature popped out of the spaceship. This one looked like a yellow jellybean, and buzzed around like a flying bloodhound, as if it were trying to sniff out the neighborhood. In a second, it had found Peter and Lucy and called the spacemen over.

There was no use hiding any longer. Peter took a deep breath and stood up. "Hi, I'm Peter," he said hopefully. Maybe they would be friendly. "That's Lucy. I live

here. . . . Oh, I guess you don't understand."

The tallest spaceman looked down at Peter. "That is not so," he said in a funny, flat voice. "We are equipped to identify, understand, and speak all known languages. Hello. How do you do? I am fine. My name is Amalthor."

"Uh, I'm fine, too," said Peter.

The smallest spaceman took up the conversation. "Hello. How do you do? I am fine. My name is Lexicon," he said. "About two thousand years ago, Earth time—but last week, our time—there appeared in the heavens over many worlds a great star. Can you explain this?"

"Two thousand years ago?" Peter asked. "Wait! I know, that was the Star of Bethlehem."

The three space visitors looked at each other. They seemed confused. "Hello. How do you do? I am fine. My name is Plutox," the third said. "We don't understand. Our mission is to search for the meaning of that star."

"You must mean Christmas. Did you come for Christmas?"

"Christmas? What is Christmas?"

"That star you saw shone over Bethlehem because Jesus was born there. He was very special. We celebrate his birthday every year with love, peace, and caring for others. That's Christmas."

"Then that is what we came for," said Amalthor."

"Well, come on, we'll show you!" cried Peter.

Lucy quacked loudly. She thought it was a good idea, too.

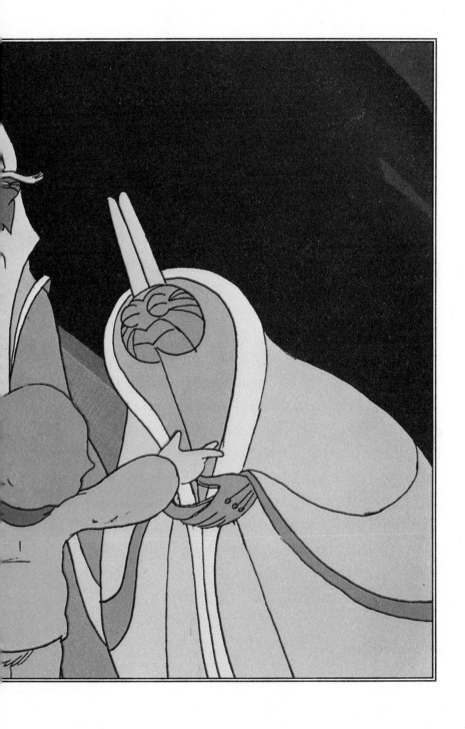

Peter decided to take his three new friends into town. They would certainly be able to discover the meaning of Christmas there. But he warned them to stay out of sight in the shadows. He knew that even on Christmas Eve some people might be scared if they saw the strangers.

The spacemen glided across the snow after Peter. They left no footprints and made no sounds. When they got to town, they stayed back against the buildings until they looked like the shadows themselves.

Soon they came to Bumble's Department Store. Peter pointed to a Christmas scene in the window. The spacemen came close to look at it. Plutox's eyes began to go *click, click, click,* just like a camera. Wow, thought Peter, what a neat way to take pictures.

Just then, Mr. Bumble came out and locked the front door. He seemed furious about something. "Bah!" he muttered. "So Gumble's thinks it can put on a better Christmas sale than Bumble's, does it? I'll show them! This means war! Christmas, humbug!" He kicked the door, shook his fist in the air, and stomped off.

The visitors watched him walk away. "Is this love, Peter?" asked Lexicon. Peter felt embarrassed. He shook his head. Then he got a bright idea. He would take them down to the town hall. Police Chief Snerk and the mayor would show them what Christmas was all about.

They slipped through the darkening streets until they reached the town hall. Peeking in through the open door, they saw the mayor in Chief Snerk's office. He appeared excited about something. The telephone rang, and the chief answered.

"Snerk here. . . . Don't tell me, you want to report a spaceship. . . . Yes, ma'am. Little green men. I'll look into it." He hung up, shaking his head. "That's the sixth call today. Has everybody gone nuts?"

"As mayor of this town," the mayor shouted, "I say, KEEP CALM!!! EVERYONE KEEP CALM!!!!! How many men have you got on duty tonight?"

"Just yours truly. I gave Barney and Herman the weekend off. It's Christmas, you know."

"Christmas Schlismas. Call 'em back—

no, no, better not. I don't want to start a panic.''

"We'd better go check into this," said the chief wearily.

"Right," agreed the mayor. "You go. I'll stay here."

"Yes, sir. If they come here—"

"COME HERE? You mean they might COME HERE? Right. We'd better go check this out. HELP! SPACEMEN!!!!"

Amalthor turned to Peter and asked, "Is this peace, Peter?"

"No," Peter admitted. He felt discouraged. Where was Christmas?

They went up the street. A bell was ringing. That was more like it. Santa Joe was standing on the corner ringing his bell.

"Merry Christmas. Help the unfortunates." He called to a group of ragged–looking boys and girls.

"Are you kidding?" They shouted back. "We are the unfortunates." Sounds of laughter rang out. It was Tough Marvin and his gang. They lived down in the poor section of town, and they were the toughest, meanest kids around. They were hanging around in the alley, and laughing and making fun of Christmas.

"What're you guys having for Christmas dinner?" one of them asked.

"Same as usual—nothin'," the next replied.

"Jeez," laughed the first. "I'm having banana pie with whipped cream and cherries, and three kinds of Jell-O, and baked potatoes, and roast goose. . . ."

The others laughed and hooted and started throwing things. Suddenly Marvin stood up. "Hang on!" he said. "What did you say?"

"Uh, roast goose?"

"Yeah." A sneaky, hungry look came into Marvin's eyes. "I wouldn't mind some of that for Christmas. And I know where we might be able to get some."

Outside, Lucy gave a weak quack. She walked quickly away, looking very upset.

"Is this caring for others, Peter?" asked Plutox.

"No," said Peter. He didn't know what to say. Wasn't there any place where people were happy at Christmas?

The clock on the town hall began to chime once more. This time it rang out six o'clock. Oh, my gosh, thought Peter. I've got to get home. Home! That was it. Why hadn't he thought of that before? He'd take the visitors home to see Christmas.

They hurried across the quiet fields toward his house. It was already dark. Peter ran through the gate, up the front steps, and burst into the hall. "Hey, everybody," he called. "Come quick. It's me. I've got a surprise."

"Peter," said his father sternly, "you're late."

"Sorry," said Peter. "But I met these— uh—people. They're strangers. I brought them home for dinner."

"What?" cried his mother. "Peter! How many times have I told you not to talk to—"

All at once she turned and saw the strangers. That stopped her talking. Her eyes grew very wide. So did Peter's father's eyes. He dropped the decoration he was holding. Even Grandma, who almost never got flustered, let go of her knitting and just stared.

"Hello. How do you do? I am fine," said

Amalthor. "Our mission is peaceful. We have come in search of the meaning of the Star of Bethlehem."

But the grown-ups just kept staring at the visitors. Peter's father glanced toward his hunting rifle.

"No, you don't understand!" cried Peter. "They came for Christmas!"

There was another long silence. Finally, Grandma stood up and approached the strangers. "Oh. Men from Mars. Well, isn't that nice," she said. "Come in, come in."

Peter wanted to hug her. At last he had found someone who had the true spirit of Christmas.

"We'll need more wood for the fire, Peter," Grandma said. "You and Lucy go get some."

When they went out, neither of them noticed that a pair of eyes was staring out at them from behind the woodpile. Someone was back there—watching them. Someone who had a reason to keep hidden.

Peter carried the wood back into the house. He looked at the Christmas tree and the decorations. They were all right, but the tree wasn't very big or very well decorated this year.

"Grandma, tell them what Christmas used to be like in the old days," Peter begged. That would give them the right idea, he thought.

The spacemen turned toward Grandma.

"Oh, my," she began. "When I was a young girl, Christmas was the happiest time of year for everyone. My father would search for a tree in the forest and bring it home, and it would touch the ceiling. We made all our own decorations in those days—stringing popcorn, tying little bows on the limbs of the trees, cutting out paper angels—it was so beautiful."

"You mean like this?" Amalthor asked.

He seemed to concentrate. Suddenly a tall tree appeared in the middle of the room. Then strings of popcorn, and paper angels, and gingerbread men, and candy canes, and red ribbons jumped out of nowhere and hung themselves on the tree. And on the top a silver star formed. The fire in the fireplace flared up, casting a warm red glow all over the room.

"Wow!" Peter exclaimed. "It's like magic!"

Grandma was really remembering now. "The whole room was decorated with branches of fir, and mistletoe hung from the doorways, and Mother would spend days in the kitchen, baking cakes and puddings. And we would all make pies, and ham, and turkey, and stuffing. . . ."

Amalthor concentrated again. Suddenly

the room became filled with all the decorations Grandma had remembered, and on the table appeared all the delicious foods they used to make for Christmas. The smell drifted through the room, making everyone hungry. Peter could hardly keep from sitting down and starting to eat.

"That's it!" cried Grandma. "That's the way Christmas used to be!" She looked as happy as Peter had ever seen her.

All at once, a terrible squawk was heard. It came from outside.

"That's Lucy!" shouted Peter. "Something's happened!" As soon as he said that, everything—the tree, the decorations, and the food—disappeared as quickly as it had come. The magic dream was over!

Peter rushed outside. Where was Lucy? There she was—and Tough Marvin had her! That pair of watching eyes had belonged to him. He had not been kidding about wanting roast goose for supper. He had Lucy by the neck and was pedaling furiously down the road on his beat-up old bike. Peter raced after him.

"Peter! Come back!" called his father. But Peter did not even turn around. His father threw on a coat and rushed after Peter. A moment later, his mother, and Grandma, and Jellybean, and the three visitors, who looked quite puzzled by all this, started out after the others. By now, Peter was practically out of sight.

Meanwhile, Chief Snerk and the mayor, followed by some of the braver townspeople, were standing at the edge of Willis Pond, looking up at the strange spaceship. Or rather, the chief was. The rest of them, especially the mayor, were hiding behind the chief. "Listen, you Martians—or whatever you are. This is the chief of police speaking. Come out of there right now!"

Of course, nothing happened.

"Maybe they can't hear you," someone suggested.

"Maybe they don't have ears."

"Of course they have ears. KEEP CALM!!!" shouted the mayor.

Just then, they heard a loud squawking and squealing behind them. It was Marvin, zooming by with Lucy. He had left the road and was trying to get away through the woods.

The chief watched him pass by, scratched his head, and turned back to the spaceship. "All right, you guys," he said firmly. "Open up in the name of the law!"

Again, nothing happened. Except that, behind them, Peter came running by. "Stop!" he shouted at Marvin.

The chief scratched his head again. Things were getting nuttier every minute.

Finally he turned back to the ship. "This is your last chance," he warned. "Or you're under arrest." He hoped that would scare them. Because he was not sure exactly how to arrest a spaceship.

Just at that moment Peter's dad rushed by. "Stop, thief!" he cried.

The chief's ears pricked up. "A robbery? Now that's more like it!" He pointed a stern finger at the spaceship. "You stay right here until I get back," he ordered. Then he blew his police whistle. "After that thief!" he shouted. In a flash, everyone had joined in the chase after Marvin and Peter and Peter's dad.

Snow had started to fall. Lots of it. Peter could barely see Marvin up ahead. Luckily, the snow made it hard for Marvin to go fast. And Lucy's squirming and squealing slowed him down even more. Where was Marvin going, anyway? Didn't he know that path led straight to the lake?

The truth was that Marvin had lost his way. He had not expected to be chased—especially not by half the town. For the first time, he was afraid. He pedaled harder and harder. Suddenly his front tire hit a frozen patch. The bike went flying into the air, crashed through a bunch of bulrushes, and spilled him head over heels out onto the frozen lake. He skidded wildly across the ice—until all at once the ice split under him. Marvin plunged through the crack into the freezing water. Lucy quickly flew up to safety.

"Help!" Marvin screamed. "Save me!"

"Hang on, Marvin, I'm coming!" Peter called. "Just hold on!"

Peter edged out toward the center of the lake. If only the ice would be solid . . .

"Help!" Marvin screamed again.

Peter crept out toward the split in the ice. He lay down and stretched out his hand. "Over here, Marvin. Grab my hand!"

Marvin reached for Peter's hand. But before he grabbed it, the ice cracked under Peter, and he, too, went crashing into the black water.

By now, Peter's dad and the chief and the rest had reached the shore. "Quick! Form a chain!" ordered the chief. The people held hands, forming a line that went out from the

shore toward the struggling boys. But it didn't stretch far enough!

"We need more people!" cried Peter's dad.

The chief looked around. There weren't any more people—except for those three strangers watching from the bank. "You there," he shouted. "C'mon. Help!"

"He is calling us," said Amalthor.

"Please," Grandma pleaded. "Help us."

"What is help?" asked Plutox.

"It means giving aid to others, I think," said Amalthor.

"Perhaps that is the meaning of Christmas."

"That is possible," said Lexicon thoughtfully. "But you know the rules forbid us to interfere."

"Yes, but this may be the way we can really learn about Christmas," put in Amalthor. "I don't care about the rules. I'm going to help." He glided past the other two out toward the end of the chain. Plutox and Lexicon looked fearfully at each other. Then they hurried off after Amalthor.

In a moment they had clasped hands with Peter's dad at the end of the line and were stretching out toward the boys. A second later, Amalthor's strong fingers had wrapped around Peter's freezing wrist and he had pulled Peter and Marvin to safety. Lucy quacked her head off. That meant "Thank goodness."

"Are you all right?" asked Peter's mother anxiously.

"I think so," Peter replied. "J-J-J-J-Just a

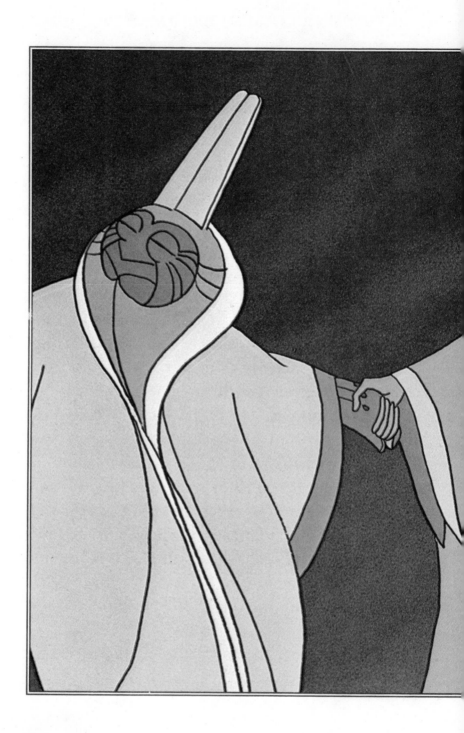

l-l-l-l-little cold." He and Marvin stood shivering on the bank.

"What about him?" asked one of the townspeople, pointing to Marvin. "He ought to be ashamed of himself, stealing that goose. And on Christmas Eve, too."

"He ought to be in jail!" said someone else.

"Right! With the key thrown away!" agreed a third.

"Arrest him, Chief. Lock him up!"

"Wait!" said Amalthor. "There is something we do not understand. Why did he steal the goose?"

"Because he's no good!"

"Because he's mean!"

Marvin was still shaking from the cold. When he heard the townspeople, he looked even more miserable than before.

Grandma stepped forward and put her arm around him. "Maybe he did it because he's hungry," she said softly.

"But how could someone go hungry if this is Christmas?" asked Plutox.

The townspeople looked at each other. They did not know what to say.

"Because we were so busy thinking about ourselves, we never stopped to think about people who have less than we do," Grandma answered finally.

"That is possible," said Amalthor.

The townspeople knew it was more than possible. It was true. They hadn't thought about anyone but themselves for a long time. And they were ashamed of themselves.

"Would you like to spend Christmas with us, Marvin?" asked Peter's mother.

"Or with us?" asked some other people.

"Aw, who're you kidding?" replied Marvin.

But they weren't kidding. The visitors' questions made the townspeople remember what Christmas is all about. They all got together and decided to have one big party. Families offered to bring extra food so Marvin and his gang could enjoy a real Christmas dinner. And the children decided that they could easily share some of their presents.

At first, Marvin was suspicious. Nobody had ever given him anything before. Nobody had ever even been nice to him before. But in the end, they convinced him. When the chief

offered to give him a ride home, he didn't even think it was a trick. And he promised to get his gang to come to the party, too.

Before he left, Marvin went up to Peter and Lucy. "Sorry about goosenapping your pet," he said.

"That's okay," said Peter. "See you at the party."

Lucy quacked. She forgave him, too.

The Chief of Police Snerk asked, "Are there any more questions?"

"No, I think we understand Christmas now," said Amalthor.

So Chief Snerk closed his notebook and announced that the case was closed.

That night they held the biggest and best Christmas party anyone had ever seen. Everyone came to help put up decorations, and everyone shared what they had with everyone else. Marvin and his gang didn't have anything to bring, but they helped put things up. And they certainly helped eat the food. They really stuffed themselves. Finally the mayor told them they didn't need to eat everything all at once. Because, he promised,

from now on, no one would ever go hungry in his town.

Everyone had such a good time that no one noticed the space visitors had left—until Peter happened to glance out the window. "Look!" he cried, pointing to the sky.

The spaceship was slowly rising into the heavens. "Good-bye," the townspeople called. "Merry Christmas—and thank you."

They weren't sure at first that the visitors had heard them. Then, suddenly, the whole

sky seemed to explode into a shower of shining stars. And, as they watched, the stars formed themselves into the shape of an angel—just like one of the paper angels Grandma had made. It rose higher and higher, until it had climbed so high no one could see it any longer.

But they would never forget what it meant.

SONGS

Why Don't They Look to the Stars

Words and music by Sylvia Tyson

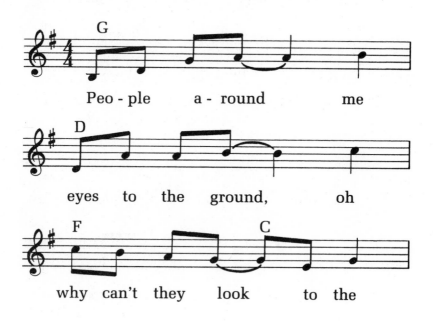

Peo - ple a - round me

eyes to the ground, oh

why can't they look to the

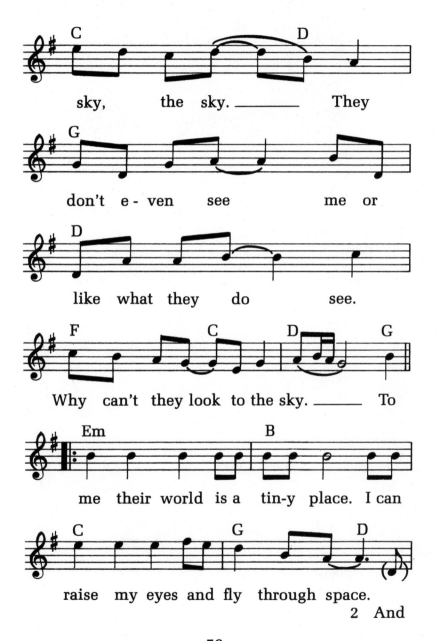

sky,   the sky. _____   They

don't e - ven   see   me or

like what they   do   see.

Why can't they look to the sky. _____ To

me   their world is a   tin-y place. I can

raise my eyes and fly through space.

2 And

1 Aren't there more like me.
   there   are more like me.

Can't they see what I _____ see.
They   see what I _____ see.

Why don't they look   to the
We   all can look   to the

stars. _____   _____   2 To
stars. _____   _____

The Way that Christmas Used to Be

Words and music by Sylvia Tyson

Time rolls fast and time rolls slow. We

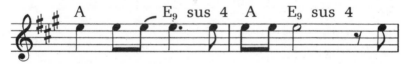

had so much so long a-go.   So

long a- go when I was young; Those

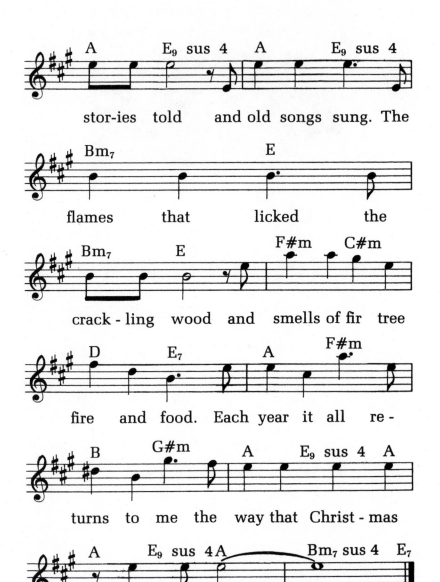

stor-ies told　and old songs sung. The

flames　that　licked　the

crack - ling　wood　and　smells of fir　tree

fire　and　food. Each year it all　re -

turns　to　me　the　way that Christ - mas

used　to　be.